Fairy Magic

bookoli

It was a beautiful sunny morning
in Springhill fairy village.

Saffron and Lacey the ladybug were
busy eating their breakfast,
when there was a loud knock
on the door.

BANG!
BANG!

"Urgent delivery from the palace!"

came a voice from outside.

"A delivery from the palace?"

said Saffron, in surprise.

"Come on Lacey, let's go outside and find out what it is!"

There was an invitation to a **party** at the palace waiting on Saffron's doorstep.

Lacey **buzzed** and did a **loop-the-loop** with excitement.

"Wow ... but that's tonight," said Saffron.
"Let's get to the library, quick!

I need to find a spell to magic up a ballgown."

The library was filled with **hundreds** and **hundreds** of dusty spellbooks.

"Where can I find a spellbook about ballgowns?"
Saffron asked the librarian, Teasel.

"Aha, I know just the one," said Teasel. "It's bright red.
Now where did I put it..."

Teasel searched through the shelves and soon found the book.

"Thank you!" said Saffron.
"Come on, Lacey. Let's go to the
Flower Garden to read the spell."

The spell was full of **strange** and **unusual** ingredients.

Glimmering Ballgown

You will need:

1 rose petal

3 drops of glimmer potion

1 oak leaf

a sprinkle of sugar

1 mouse whisker

10 silver sequins

Throw the ingredients into the river at sunset while saying,

"Rose and shine, brown oak leaf,
Whisker, sequin, sugar sweet.
Make my glimmering gown complete."

Lacey **waved** her legs and pointed to the flower bed.
"Well done, Lacey!" laughed Saffron.

"You found a **rose**! That's our first ingredient.
Let's go to the science lab next to find glimmer potion."

The lab was full of fairies **mixing**, **measuring**, and **inventing**. Best of all, it was run by Saffron's auntie, **Saffia**.

"Do you have some **glimmer** potion?" Saffron asked Aunt Saffia.

"We've just made a fresh batch," said Aunt Saffia.

"Help yourself!"

Saffron put the glimmer potion in her magic pocket.

Next on her list was to find an

oak leaf.

Saffron and Lacey **flapped**
their wings and flew far away to the
Whispering Wood.
"We're running out of time,"
said Saffron, quickly picking an
oak leaf.
"What's our next ingredient?"

Lacey **buzzed** over to the Treetop Fairy Cafe.

"That's right!" remembered Saffron.

"Sugar! We can get a sprinkle of sugar from the cafe."

CAFE

The cafe was run by Saffron's friend, Dandelion.

"You look like you're in a rush," he said.

"I'm doing a ballgown spell," Saffron told him, "and I need to find
a sprinkle of sugar,
a mouse whisker,
and ten silver
sequins
before dusk."

"Here's your sugar," said Dandelion.
"Try the animal hospital to find the whisker."

"Why didn't I think of that!"
said Saffron, racing outside.

"Thank you!"

Saffron's dad, Ash, was a nurse at the animal hospital.

"You're in luck," he said. "We have a collection of mouse whiskers.

They're very useful for healing spells."

"Thanks, Dad," said Saffron.

"We've almost got everything now."

But it was getting late. Saffron still needed to find the **sequins** and get to the river **before sunset**, otherwise her spell wouldn't work.

Saffron and Lacey **flapped** their wings and **flew** through the sky to Fairy School.

The little fairies in Miss Marigold's class were so cute! But Saffron couldn't stop and play with them today.

"Do you have any **sequins** in the craft corner, please?"
Saffron asked her old teacher, Miss Marigold.

"Fairy schools always have sequins,"
smiled Miss Marigold.

"Are you collecting ingredients for a **ballgown** spell?
That **door** over there will take you to the **river**..."

The sun was setting
as **Saffron** and
Lacey reached the river.
Saffron took a **deep breath**
and threw the ingredients into the water.
"Rose and shine, brown oak leaf,
Whisker, sequin, sugar sweet.
Make my glimmering gown **complete**."

There was a **shimmer** in the air and a burst of **beautiful music.**
When Saffron looked down, she saw that she was wearing
the most wonderful ballgown.

"It worked!" she cried. "Lacey, let's go to the ball!"

That night
at the ball, there seemed to be some
special magic in Saffron's ballgown.
It made her feet **light** and every **twirl** was perfect.
She **danced** and **spun** and **whirled**
until the clock struck midnight.

Yawning, Saffron and Lacey
made their way out of the palace gates.

"I wish there could be
a ball every day," said Lacey.

"It was **amazing**. But I'm not sure I'd want to go
to a ball **every** day," smiled Saffron. "Making ballgowns is
really hard work!"

The End